PUFFIN BOOKS

Jimmy Woods and the Big Bad Wolf

Mick Gowar has worked as a journalist, a
PR Executive and a college lecturer. He
now devotes all his time to writing,
particularly poetry and songs, and is a
lively performer of his own work. He lives
in Cambridge.

Barry Wilkinson worked in the fields of
stained glass, animation, graphics and
design before concentrating on illustration.
He even designed and made the Regent
Street Christmas decorations one year! He
has illustrated many children's books as
well as doing drawings for many of the
Jackanory stories.

THE DAY MATT SOLD GREAT GRANDMA
  Eleanor Allen and Jane Cope
CLIVE AND THE MISSING FINGER
  Sarah Garland
MADAM SIZZERS Sarah Garland
THE REAL PORKY PHILIPS Mark Haddon
WILF, THE BLACK HOLE AND THE POISONOUS MARIGOLD Hiawyn Oram
  and Dee Shulman
THE BLOB Tessa Potter and Peter Cottrill
SPOOKED Philip Wooderson and Jane
  Cope

CHILLERS

Jimmy Woods and the Big Bad Wolf

Mick Gowar

Illustrated by

Barry Wilkinson

PUFFIN BOOKS

PUFFIN BOOKS

Published by the Penguin Group
Penguin Books Ltd, 27 Wrights Lane, London W8 5TZ, England
Penguin Books USA Inc., 375 Hudson Street, New York, New York 10014, USA
Penguin Books Australia Ltd, Ringwood, Victoria, Australia
Penguin Books Canada Ltd, 10 Alcorn Avenue, Toronto, Ontario, Canada M4V 3B2
Penguin Books (NZ) Ltd, 182–190 Wairau Road, Auckland 10, New Zealand

Penguin Books Ltd, Registered Offices: Harmondsworth, Middlesex, England

First published by A & C Black (Publishers) Ltd 1994
Published in Puffin Books 1995
10 9 8 7 6 5 4

Made and printed in Great Britain by William Clowes Ltd, Beccles and London

Chapter One

Jimmy Woods was the worst kind of bully. He didn't do it to look tough or hard; he did it because he was greedy and because he liked hurting people.

Jimmy Woods wasn't that big, but you could never be sure where he would stop.

All the kids in our street were terrified of Jimmy Woods. He would bully anyone.

Have you ever seen those adverts that builders and plumbers put in the newspapers or in shop windows?

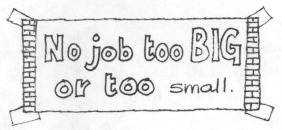

No job too BIG or too small.

That was what Jimmy Woods was like. It didn't matter if you were a three year old shrimp or a third year at the Comprehensive, Jimmy Woods would have a go at you.

Saturday morning was his favourite time: the pocket money rush hour to the corner shop at the bottom of the hill.

Jimmy Woods had a knack of appearing out of nowhere, as if he'd been beamed down from a spaceship. I don't know how he did it.

Every Saturday, for me, was a losing battle with Jimmy Woods. I'd come out of my front gate and look up and down the road to make sure the coast was clear, but as soon as I started running down the hill to the shop: WHAMO! Before I was half-way there, Jimmy Woods materialized by the post box.

Hang on a minute. I want a word with you.

Ev-hello, J-Jimmy.

Where are you going in such a hurry?

Ev-nowhere Jimmy.

Nowhere? You can't be going nowhere. You must be going somewhere, there's no such place as nowhere. I think you're going to the shop to buy sweets — aren't you?

N-n-no Jimmy.

Are you lying to me?

N-n-no Jimmy.

7

I'd try my best to keep my fist clenched, but Jimmy always managed to prise it open.

"Ah-ha! Fifty pee! That's your pocket money, isn't it? So you *were* going to the shop to buy sweets, weren't you – eh?" And he'd let go of my hand and grab my ear and twist.

"Weren't you?"

"Y-y-yes, Jimmy."

"So you did lie to me, didn't you?"

Another twist of the ear.

"Owww! Y-y-yes, Jimmy."

"Then I'd better take that fifty pee to teach you a lesson. *Never* lie to me again!"

And Jimmy would laugh and laugh, as I ran all the way home trying not to let him see me crying.

Chapter Two

How did Jimmy Woods get away with it?
Well, the main reason was that the
grown-ups didn't take him seriously,
even though the kids were frightened of
him. Maybe it was because he didn't look
like a typical bully. He was more lean and
lanky, not the gorilla-type at all. Maybe
they had other, 'more important' things
on their minds — like unemployment, or
the hole in ozone layer. I don't know.
My parents were typical.
When I told Mum,
she just said,

Well, that'll teach
you not to play with
boys like Jimmy
Woods.

Play! Didn't she realize that this was no game?

My Dad seemed to think that Jimmy Woods was one of life's little nuisances, like the measles or a leaky tap in the kitchen.

"You've got to learn to stand up for yourself, son," he said.

It was same with the other parents. They acted as if it was *our* fault for not being as mean and spiteful and nasty as Jimmy Woods.

And Jimmy Woods might have got away with it for years and years – if it hadn't been for Prince.

No. Not the popstar. Prince is my family's German Shepherd dog. And one day I found out that Jimmy Woods was petrified of Prince.

It was a Saturday morning. Pocket money day. I'd been watching Jimmy Woods and his little ways. I'd worked out that if I got to the shop really early, there was a good chance I could miss Jimmy Woods. (He was a lazy so-and-so. He didn't like getting up in the morning – even if it meant he'd have to miss out on the odd fifty pee.)

I was just going out of the door, when Dad called me back.

Take Prince with you. He could do with a walk.

"Do I have to, Dad," I moaned. "You know what Prince is like. He has to stop at every lamp-post, every tree *and* every gatepost. It'll take *hours*." (I was worried that if I wasn't quick, I'd run into Jimmy Woods.)

It was no good. Dad just gave me a real nagging, "You treat this place like a hotel. You never wash-up, or make your bed, or . . ." Well, you know the kind of thing.

13

Although Prince made all his usual stops, we got to the shop safely. But on the way back — there was Jimmy Woods. Prince was having a good sniff round the post box, so I guess Jimmy didn't see him straight away.

"Hullo, hullo, hullo," said Jimmy Woods. "What have we here? A little shrimp with a bag full of goodies!"

I was just about to say something when Prince stuck his head, and then the rest of his body, round the post box. He stared at Jimmy Woods, and I could see from Prince's eyes that it was hate-at-first-sight.

Jimmy Woods turned white.

Jimmy Woods – big, tough Jimmy Woods
– was shaking with fear.

"I'm going to report you to the law," said
Jimmy Woods, backing away as fast as he
could. "Vicious brutes like that . . . they
. . . they . . . need shooting!"

And as quickly as he'd appeared, Jimmy
Woods was gone.

Now although Prince is big and looks like a wolf, he's really as soft as a jam doughnut. My Dad trained Prince really well. He can walk to heel and all the usual things, but he's also got a special trick – he can sit *amazingly* still. If you say "Stay Prince!" he won't move a muscle until you tell him to, not even if you wave a big juicy bone under his nose.

In fact, there's only one thing that drives Prince absolutely wild: his dog whistle.

Do you know what a dog whistle is? It's a
special whistle that makes a note so high
that only a dog can hear it. My dad
bought it when Prince was a puppy. But
the first time he blew it, Prince went
bonkers! He leapt about three feet in the
air, howled like a werewolf, then hurtled
out of the door as if all the fiends of hell
were after him!

It must be like having an instant headache.

So we all agreed that we'd never blow it
again.

But Jimmy Woods didn't know Prince
was a big softie. Jimmy Woods was scared
stiff of Prince.

From that day on, I always took Prince down to the corner shop with me on Saturdays. Pretty soon, all the kids in the street noticed that Jimmy Woods never bothered me when Prince was there.

We soon had a Saturday morning convoy: Prince, me and all the other kids, going down to the corner shop to spend our pocket money.

Thanks to Prince, Jimmy Woods' days as the local bully were over . . . or so we thought.

But we were wrong.

Chapter Three

It was a Tuesday afternoon –
I remember it clearly – just
after tea; Mum was pulling
the curtains, when she
suddenly called out, "Come
and look, everybody!
You'll never believe who's
coming out of
Granny Timpson's house."

Me and Dad went to the
window and who should
we see but . . . Jimmy Woods!

He was walking down the
front path. As he got to the
gate, he turned back
and yelled,

And then he laughed.

"Well, well!" said Mum. "Who would have thought it. Jimmy Woods, the good neighbour."

But there was something about the way he laughed which I didn't like. I'd heard him laugh like that before – when he was taking sweets or money from me. It was a hard laugh; the opposite of a real laugh. It was a threat, a nasty promise.

That week we saw Jimmy Woods come out of Granny Timpson's two or three more times. And each time he said the same thing, "Thank you *so* much for having me." Then he did his nasty laugh.

I was getting worried for old Granny, but Mum didn't think there was anything wrong.

I think it's nice that she's got someone visiting her. She's too old to be in that house on her own. She'd be better off in a home, but you know what she's like.

I'd better explain about Granny. Despite her nickname, Granny Timpson was *not* a sweet little old lady. She was little and old, but she was very bad-tempered. She hated people fussing.

A couple of times the previous winter, Mum and I had knocked on her door to check she was alright.

It wouldn't have been so bad, but we'd been *asked* to keep an eye on her by the District Nurse. Nurse Proctor was an old friend of Mum's.

Would you keep an eye on Mrs Timpson? She's not as strong as she thinks. I know she's rude and awkward, but she's frightened. She thinks if she starts asking for help, she'll be forced to go into a home.

I thought about that now. Granny Timpson certainly didn't look very strong. Jimmy Woods *was* strong, and nasty. I didn't like the look of it at all. I decided it was time to check up on Granny – but this time, on my own.

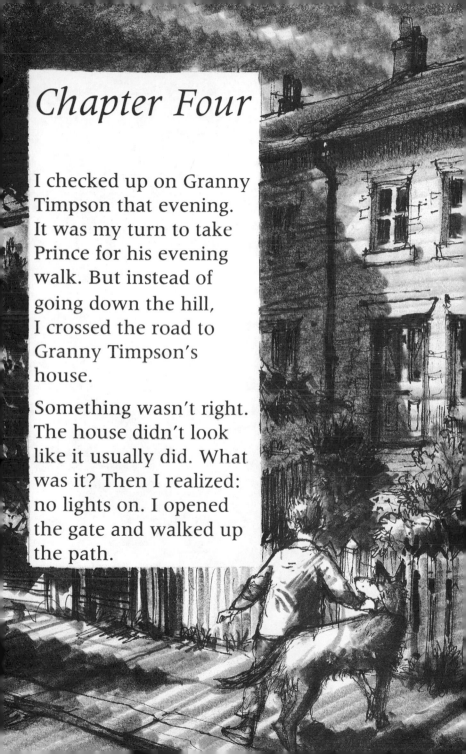

Chapter Four

I checked up on Granny Timpson that evening. It was my turn to take Prince for his evening walk. But instead of going down the hill, I crossed the road to Granny Timpson's house.

Something wasn't right. The house didn't look like it usually did. What was it? Then I realized: no lights on. I opened the gate and walked up the path.

As I got to the front door I heard strange sounds coming from the other side, like someone or something snuffling and every so often gulping for breath. It sounded like a small dog. But Granny Timpson didn't have any animals, I knew that.

Then I realized that the sounds I could hear weren't animal sounds at all. Someone on the other side of the door was crying. It wasn't very loud, but it was definitely crying.

I knocked on the door. The crying stopped. I knocked again. No reply. I bent down and lifted the flap of the letter box.

Hello, Mrs Timpson, are you alright?

There was a scuffling sound. And then
Granny called out

Go away!
Haven't you
done enough,
you wicked
boy!

"It's not him, Granny, it's me – Ben, from
over the road. What's the matter,
Granny?"

"I'm not telling you. I'm not opening the
door – not to any boys. I'm finished with
boys. You're all wicked! Wicked, wicked,
wicked!"

"But, Granny . . ."

It was no good. I don't know what would
have happened if my big sister Debbie
hadn't come along just at that moment.

I hadn't heard her coming up the path. She was on her way out to meet her mates. She was wearing the skirt my dad says looks as if it's been painted on.

"It's Granny Timpson," I said. "Something's going on – Jimmy Woods. I don't know what, and she won't speak to me."

"Let me try," said Debbie. "You go and wait by the gate. If something *has* been going on, the sight of Prince will probably give her a heart attack!"

I led Prince back up the path. Debbie bent down and started speaking through the letter box.

It took about ten minutes, but eventually Granny Timpson opened the door and peered out. Debbie started to go inside, so I went to follow. Debbie turned round and shook her head.

"No!" she said sternly. "You two – *stay*!"

Chapter Five

I don't know how long Prince
and I waited there. It felt like
hours. But we're obedient,
Prince and I. We hadn't been
told to go; we'd been told to
stay, so we stayed.

Eventually, Debbie came back
to the front door and
beckoned us in. I'd never been
in Granny Timpson's house
before. It wasn't very nice.
The paper in the hall was a
dingy yellow colour and all
the paintwork was a nasty
dark brown. The whole place
smelled of boiled fish.

Granny was in the sitting
room, in an old rocking
chair. The light overhead
was dim and the fire in the old
grate was out. The room was
cold and dark and miserable.

I sat down on an old grey sofa next to Debbie.

"You were right," she said. "That thug Jimmy Woods *has* been up to no good . . ." And she leaned across and patted Granny's hand which was resting on the arm of the rocking chair.

"He took my back-door key," said Granny. "Comes and goes as he pleases."

Helps himself to tea and biscuits. I haven't been able to get out - not even to get my pension. That's what he's after. He said he's coming back tomorrow, and I'd better have it when he arrives!

"Why don't you tell the District Nurse — no, the Police — " I began.

Debbie shook her head and frowned at me.

"No," said Granny. "No, I can't do that. I mustn't do that. If I tell them, I know what they'll do: they'll say I can't manage on my own. They'll put me in a *home*." And she started to cry again.

Debbie shot me a glare. She went over to Granny and put her arm round her. What had *I* done wrong? It seemed the only thing to do.

Granny gave a kind of a shudder and pulled herself together. "I'm not leaving my home because of the likes of *him*!" she said. I could see her point, but . . .

I couldn't think of anything to say. This was serious. This wasn't just little kids having pocket money and sweets pinched. Something had to be done – but what?

We all sat in silence.

Then Prince got up, went over to the rocking chair, and licked Granny's hand. Granny smiled for the first time that evening.

"Good boy," she said. "You can trust dogs – not like humans. Dogs will look after you."

Debbie suddenly sat up very straight.

"I think that's the answer," she said in a slow, deliberate voice. "Jimmy Woods is terrified of Prince. If we lent you Prince for a couple of days. . . ?"

She paused, then shook her head. "No," she said. "That wouldn't work. As soon as we took Prince back, Jimmy Woods would be round again. No, what we need is some way to scare Jimmy Woods so badly that he won't dare to come back — ever!"

She paused again and frowned.

I looked at Granny Timpson, then back to Debbie.

A smile slowly spread across Debbie's face. "I think I've got an idea!" she said. "It was something I saw on TV the other night. You'll probably laugh when I tell you, but I think it'll work. No! I'm *certain* it'll work!"

Chapter Six

When I look back on that day, I realize how lucky we were. Lucky to have Prince, lucky that Jimmy Woods was scared of dogs, and lucky that next day was a Saturday, no school for me and no work for Debbie.

Prince, Debbie and I were round at Granny Timpson's house by half-past eight that morning. Even so, Debbie's plan took a lot of arranging. It was almost half-past nine before we were ready.

Granny Timpson was really nervous. "It will work – won't it?" she asked.

"Don't worry, Granny," Debbie said. "Everything will be fine. You just sit here, and don't move. Everything's been taken care of . . ." But she didn't sound very sure.

Debbie closed the curtains in the sitting room. "Right," she said, "it's time for us to hide."

We squeezed into the thin gap between the sofa and the wall of Granny's sitting room.

"Have you got it ready?" she whispered. I put my hand in my pocket. My fingers touched the cold, metal tube.

"Yes," I whispered back.

"You know what to do?"

"Of course I do," I hissed.

We peeped around the end of the sofa. The figure in the rocking chair was motionless. Everything was ready.

We'd just settled down again behind the sofa when we heard Granny's front gate click open, then bang shut. Heavy boots clomped up the front path. But instead of stopping at the front door, the footsteps continued round the side of the house.

There was a rattle and click as a key turned in the back door lock, then a crash as the back door was slammed. Whoever had come in was very sure of himself.

"Yoo-hoo, Granny! You've got company," a voice called up the passageway. It was Jimmy Woods.

There was no reply.

Coo-ee Granny!

Still no reply.

That's not very friendly, Granny.

Jimmy sounded annoyed.

Still no reply.

I hope you've got the tea and biscuits ready.

said Jimmy, sounding threatening.
His voice was getting louder as he came
along the passage to the sitting room.

Or I'm going to have to huff
and puff and blow your house
down – just like the
big bad wolf !

And as he said that, he pushed open the
sitting room door with a bang.

"What's going on?" Jimmy sounded crosser than ever. "Why have you got the curtains drawn? It's dangerous having it so dark. I could fall over and hurt myself!"

Jimmy Woods looked
round the room. No
sign of Granny. Then
he saw the figure
sitting in the rocking
chair in the darkest
corner of the room.
It had a shawl
draped over its head.
It was facing away
from the door.
It was perfectly still.

And Jimmy began to creep up behind the rocking chair.

When Jimmy Woods got to the chair
three things happened.

First, Jimmy leapt into
the air and yelled:

BOO!

I pulled the dog
whistle out of
my pocket and
blew it as hard
as I could.

The figure in the shawl let out a blood-curdling howl and leapt high into the air. It landed on the floor on all fours – tensed and ready to spring.

"Aaaargh!" yelled Jimmy, backing away.

Backing away was the worst thing Jimmy Woods could have done.

And Prince leapt up at
Jimmy Woods . . .

But Prince never
touched him. With
a howl much
louder than Prince's,
Jimmy fled out of
the sitting room,
down the hall, and
out of the front door.

Debbie and I went upstairs
to the front bedroom.

Granny Timpson was still sitting in her chair.

"He's gone, Granny," Debbie said.
"I know," said Granny. "I heard. But will he be gone for good? What if he comes back?"

"He won't," said Debbie. "Not after I put the word around about how he was chased off by an old age pensioner."

Who's going to believe his story? Attacked by a wolf in Granny's clothing! He'll be laughed out of town.

"But just *in case* anything like this happens again, I've brought you a little present." Debbie rummaged in her handbag and brought out two plastic covered packets and a screw-driver.

"Chains — for the front and back doors. And make sure you use them. Don't let *anyone* in unless you know who they are." And she handed me the packets and the screwdriver. "I did all the thinking. *You* can do the practical work!"

Chapter Seven

And that was Jimmy's
career as a full-time
bully pretty much
finished. He may have
tried a few more
pocket money hold-
ups after that, but I
never heard about
them.

Just as Debbie said,
the story got around.
Jimmy Woods even
got a nickname, thanks
to Debbie: "Little Red
Riding Woods",
because he'd been
scared by a "wolf".

Debbie was right, no-one believed
Jimmy's story. Everyone started laughing
at Jimmy, even the little shrimps. And
you can't terrorize people if they crease
up every time they see you.

Bullies may laugh, and they may tell cruel jokes, but they haven't really got a sense of humour. And if there's one thing a bully can't stand it's being made fun of. They can't bear it – just like Prince can't bear the sound of a dog whistle.

Debbie and I felt a bit mean about blowing that whistle. We knew Prince couldn't stand it. But it was an emergency. And Granny Timpson wasn't the only one to get a present. We bought Prince a steak and kidney pie from the shop on the corner.

And that wasn't all; Granny Timpson bought him a pie, too.

Some other Puffin Chillers

CHILLERS

The Day Matt Sold Great-grandma

Eleanor Allen
Illustrated by
Jane Cope

It was only an old photograph. Matt thought no one would even miss it. But he soon begins to wish he had left it in the attic when his great-grandma comes back from the dead to haunt him!

CHILLERS

Clive and the Missing Finger

Sarah Garland

What has happened to Clive's strange neighbour,
the man with the missing finger? Why has he
mysteriously disappeared? And what is his guilty
secret?

CHILLERS

The Real
Porky Philips

Mark Haddon

Porky Philips is the story of a boy whom no one
really notices. Even his family can't tell the
difference between him and the mysterious
double who threatens to take his place . . .

Coming soon in Puffin Chillers

CHILLERS

The Blob

Tessa Potter
Illustrated by
Peter Cottrill

The first blob appeared on Graham's book after second break. It was a rusty red colour and it looked suspiciously like blood.

Where did the sinister blobs come from? And did they have something to do with the locked classroom upstairs, or the strange new headteacher?

CHILLERS

Madam Sizzers

Sarah Garland

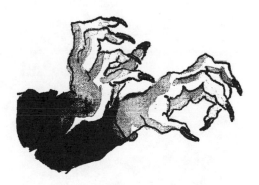

There's something creepy about Madam Sizzers.
Perhaps it's just her sharp red fingernails and her
gleaming scissors. Rachel and Lola try to annoy
her, but then they stumble upon a dark secret. . .

CHILLERS

Spooked

Philip Wooderson
Illustrated by
Jane Cope

The note said 'Please help me', and with it was a
dusty old photograph of a pale-looking girl. Pete
tried to forget them. Then he saw the face at the
window of the empty house. The same girl's face.
Who was she? Pete had to find out, and that
meant going into the house. Alone.